壮族神话传说少儿绘本

The Legend of the Zhuang Bronze Drums

壮族铜鼓的传说

编著：南宁市博物馆 / 广西霖创文化创意有限责任公司

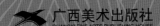

广西美术出版社
GUANGXI FINE ARTS PUBLISHING HOUSE

图书在版编目（CIP）数据

壮族铜鼓的传说：中文、英文 / 南宁市博物馆，广西霖创文
化创意有限责任公司编著. 一南宁：广西美术出版社，2020.12
（壮族神话传说少儿绘本）
ISBN 978-7-5494-2282-1

Ⅰ . ①壮… Ⅱ . ①南… ②广… Ⅲ . ①儿童文学－图画故事－
中国－当代 Ⅳ . ①I287.8

中国版本图书馆CIP数据核字（2020）第234523号

壮族铜鼓的传说

壮族神话传说少儿绘本

ZHUANGZU TONGGU DE CHUANSHUO　　ZHUANGZU SHENHUA CHUANSHUO SHAO' ER HUIBEN

编　　著：南宁市博物馆 / 广西霖创文化创意有限责任公司
主　　编：张晓剑 / 覃　忠 / 周佳璐
编　　委：刘德雨 / 吕虹霖 / 蓝　涛 / 潘昕昊 / 欧　文 / 彭　柯
　　　　　梁　晨 / 咸　安 / 夏丽娜 / 黎琼泽 / 张沥仁 / 周　怡
绘　　画：周佳璐 / 张云浩 / 王恩惠 / 冯　磊 / 李　琼
英文译者：姚小文
英文审校：[英] Judith Sovin

出　版　人：陈　明
终　　　审：邓　欣
策 划 编 辑：谭　宇
责 任 编 辑：谭　宇　黄　玲
装 帧 设 计：谭　宇
校　　　对：梁冬梅
审　　　读：肖丽新
出 版 发 行：广西美术出版社
地　　　址：广西南宁市望园路9号（邮编：530023）
网　　　址：www.gxfinearts.com
印　　　刷：广西壮族自治区地质印刷厂
版 次 印 次：2020年12月第1版第1次印刷
开　　　本：889 mm×1194 mm　1/16
印　　　张：2
字　　　数：20千字
书　　　号：ISBN 978-7-5494-2282-1
定　　　价：45.00元

传说，壮族开天辟地的老祖宗布洛陀创造了天、地和人。

Legend has it that Buluotuo—the ancient ancestor of the Zhuang people—separated the Heavens and Earth. He also created the Zhuang people.

住在天上的布洛陀
只要把头低一点点,
就能看得见地上的子孙的日子
过得是好还是坏。

Buluotuo resided in Heavens.
By lowering his head a little,
Buluotuo could see how his descendants
down on Earth were getting on.

有时他会打开天门，

看看人们还缺些什么，

就继续补造他们需要的东西。

On occasion,
he would open the gate of Heavens
to see if the people needed anything.
Buluotuo would provide them
with everything they needed.

起初，壮族人住在高山大岭上，日子过得蛮不错。

Initially, the Zhuang people lived very happily in the mountains.

慢慢地，在一些常年照不到阳光的阴暗旮旯角落，

滋生出了毒虫恶兽和妖魔鬼怪。

Slowly, poisonous creatures and demonic monsters
came into being in the shadows where the warmth
and goodness of the sun could not reach them.

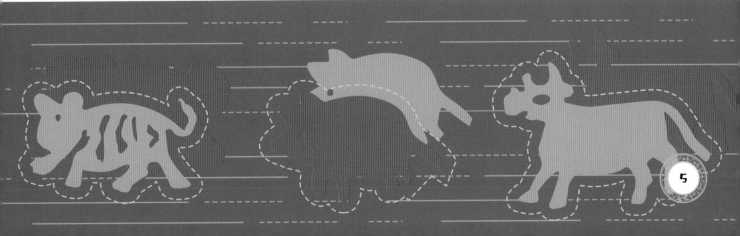

这些毒虫鬼怪一到晚上就四处乱窜，
伤害人畜，人们不得安宁。

As night fell, the monsters and foul creatures began to
come out of hiding and ravage the people and their livestock.
The poor people were terrified and had no peace.

布洛陀知道后，便来到了凡间。他对人们说："大家的灾难我已经知道了。大家说吧，要我帮忙做点什么呢？"

Seeing all these from up in Heavens, Buluotuo came down to Earth. He spoke to the people, "I can see your suffering. Let me know how I can help you."

人们齐声说：“大地上样样都好，就是缺少星星。如果你把天上的星星摘一些下来安在地上，晚上星星照亮大地，毒虫鬼怪就不敢出来，我们就得安宁了。”

The people answered in unison, "Everything on Earth is fine but there are no stars here! If you could gather some stars from the sky and plant them down on Earth, the stars would light up the Earth at night and the monsters won't dare to come out, then peace will be ours."

布洛陀想了想，笑着说："我们自己动手造星星吧。"

人们听了，十分高兴。

After some thought,
Buluotuo laughed and said, "Let us make the stars together!"
The people were thrilled with his idea.

布洛陀带领大家挖三彩泥做成模子，采孔雀石，砍青杠柴，烧炼铜水。

Buluotuo showed the people how to dig for three—coloured clay, to make moulds, and to mine malachite. He also taught the people how to cut down the big oak trees and how to boil water for copper smelting.

经过三天三夜，人们浇铸出一个圆柱状的东西。它两头圆，中间小，一头封顶一头空，身上有星星、刀箭、斧凿、鱼叉、耕织、狩猎等许多图案。

After three days and three nights of hard toil, a wide cylindrical object was cast. The object had a flat sealed end, a tapered middle and an open end. It was beautifully embellished with a multitude of patterns and images of stars, knives and arrows, axes and chisels, fish spears and all kinds of farming, weaving and hunting tools.

布洛陀笑眯眯地拎起它，用拳头朝封顶面中心的大星星一擂，顿时发出像雷一样的声响，那些躲在旮旯角落里的毒虫恶兽和妖魔鬼怪被吓得四处逃窜。

Bluotuo smiled as he picked up the object and beat the big star on the sealed end. It made a tremendous noise like thunder. This noise resonated throughout the land, terrifying the monsters and demonic creatures, and sent them scattering wildly in all directions.

人们高兴地围着布洛陀和这个金光闪闪的东西唱起歌、跳起舞来。布洛陀一边擂着它一边大声说："这个东西叫铜鼓，它就是地上的星星！它会帮你们杀死毒虫恶兽和妖魔鬼怪，保护村寨！"

The Zhuang people danced and sang with happiness circling Buluotuo and the glittering object. Beating the object, Buluotuo announced, "This object is a bronze drum. It is a star on Earth! It will kill all the demonic creatures and evil monsters, and protect you and your village!"

不久，千山万岭上的家家户户、村村寨寨，都照着布洛陀造的铜鼓的样子，造出了千千万万的铜鼓。铜鼓越造越多，多得像天上的星星一样。

Before long, every household in every village in the mountains had made many thousands of bronze drums in the image of the one Buluotuo had created. They were splendid and as numerous as the stars in the sky.

布洛陀回天上去了。人们按照他的嘱咐，依照铜鼓身上的纹饰，学会了耕种、纺织和打猎等各种本事。

Buluotuo returned to Heavens. The Zhuang people learnt many skills from the instructions that Buluotuo had inscribed in the patterns on the bronze drum. They became skilled at farming, hunting and weaving .

从此，只要发现毒虫恶兽和妖魔鬼怪，
人们就擂响铜鼓来驱散它们。

Ever since then,
wherever poisonous creatures and demonic monsters are found,
the Zhuang people beat their bronze drums to disperse them.

壮族人民喜欢在唱歌跳舞时擂响铜鼓，
踩着鼓点跳舞。

The Zhuang people love to beat bronze drums
while singing and dancing,
and to move their bodies to the beat of the bronze drums.

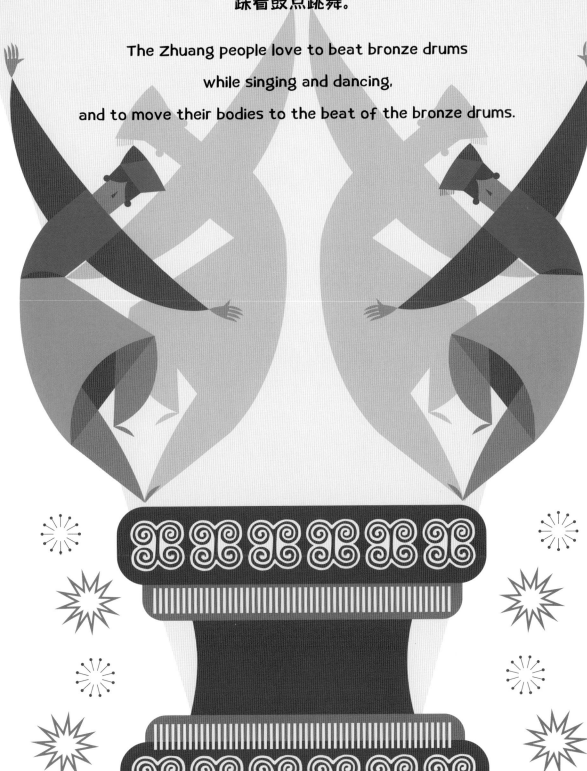

庆祝节日的时候，人们用铜鼓盛糯米饭、肥牛肉和甜米酒……

when the Zhuang people celebrate festivals, they fill their bronze drums with glutinous rice, delicious beef and good rice wine.

壮家人爱铜鼓。他们编了一首歌：

"天上星星多，地上铜鼓多；星星和铜鼓，给我们安乐。"

这首歌和布洛陀造铜鼓的传说世世代代流传下来。

The Zhuang people are very proud of their bronze drums and they sing "Blossoming stars in Heavens, blossoming bronze drums on Earth. Stars and bronze drums, offering us happiness."
This song and the legend of Buluotuo and the bronze drums have been passed down from generation to generation.